MARY STANLEY

AN ANGEL AT MY BACK

Mary Stanley is the author of five novels, *Retreat*, *Missing*, *Revenge*, *Searching for Home* and *The Lost Garden*. Her books have been widely translated. Her short stories appear in a variety of anthologies. She also writes for the *Irish Daily Mail*.

www.marystanley.com

NEW ISLAND *Open Door*

AN ANGEL AT MY BACK
First published 2008
by New Island
2 Brookside
Dundrum Road
Dublin 14

www.newisland.ie

A CIP catalogue record for this book is available from the British
Library.

ISBN 978-1-905494-86-6

New Island receives financial assistance from
The Arts Council (An Chomhairle Ealaíon), Dublin, Ireland.

Printed in Ireland by ColourBooks
Cover design by Artmark

1 3 5 4 2

Distributed By:
Grass Roots Press
Toll Free: 1-888-303-3213
Fax: (780) 413-6582
Web Site: www.literacyservices.com

Dear Reader,

On behalf of myself and the other contributing authors, I would like to welcome you to the sixth Open Door series. We hope that you enjoy the books and that reading becomes a lasting pleasure in your life.

Warmest wishes,

Patricia Scanlan.

Patricia Scanlan
Series Editor

For my daughter
Sophie Higel
with love

One

My name is Lucy. Lucy Benedict.

My dad says I have the voice of an angel. 'Lucy, sing for me,' he says.

And I sing. I love the sound of music. I can hear it inside my head. Sometimes I think I can hear it inside my bones. It moves my heart. No, it is more than that. The beat of my heart is in time with the music.

I love all music. Rap. Garage. Classical. Rock. Blues. Jazz. Opera.

'Ah, Lucy,' my dad says. 'You sound like an angel.'

'She sounds like two angels,' my mum says.

I love my mum and dad. They are the best people I know. And they love me.

And Paul.

They love Paul too. Paul is my brother. He is nearly two years older than me. He is nearly ten.

Sometimes Paul is very silly. And sometimes he is nasty. He says he remembers when I was born. Of course he can't remember when I was born. He was not quite two. So how could he remember?

He says things to annoy me.

Brothers are like that. They think they know more than their sisters. Of course they don't. But they like to think they do.

Paul is taller than me. Most people are taller than me. But my dad says if I don't smoke I will grow more.

My mum says, 'Lucy isn't stupid. Of course she won't smoke.'

I don't smoke. I don't think it's nice. But both my mum and my dad smoke.

'Parents are not always right,' my mum says. 'I know you must learn from us. You must learn from the things we do. But sometimes we do things you must not do. Smoking is one of those things.'

My dad and my mum smoke in the garden. They go outside even when it's raining or snowing. They don't want Paul or me to smoke. I know that. I won't ever smoke.

Sometimes Paul steals a cigarette from my mum's handbag. Then he slips out into the garden. He hides behind the apple tree. He tries to smoke the cigarette. But he coughs and coughs.

Then he stubs the cigarette out and throws it over the wall.

★

Last summer Paul tied me up in the garden. He tied me to the apple tree with a piece of clothesline. He left me there while he went inside to fetch his toy gun. We were playing war.

Again.

Paul's war game was not much fun. It was always the same. He chased me around our garden, around the apple tree and then across the grass. Our garden is not very big. He always caught me at the same place – in the middle of the grass as I tried to get back to the apple tree. He was able to climb the apple tree but I was not. My arms were not strong enough to pull me up, no matter how hard I tried.

He caught me on the grass. He threw himself at me in a rugby tackle and knocked me to the ground. Then he dragged me to the apple tree. And he accused me of being a coward.

'You will be shot at dawn,' he said.

He wound the clothesline around and around me so that I could not move.

'You're hurting me,' I said.

'Don't worry. It won't be for long,' Paul said. 'I'll get my gun and shoot you. Then you won't feel a thing.'

He set off down the garden to the house.

'Paul, come back,' I called. But he could not hear me because he had already gone indoors.

'Paul,' I called again.

Mum had gone to the shops and Dad was at work. I had to wait until Paul came back and shot me with his water pistol.

It was hot in the garden. I wished he would hurry up. My back hurt and my arms were pulled around the tree behind me. I could not move.

'Hurry up,' I called. I could smell the apples in the tree. I like apple tart. My mum makes nicer ones than you can

5

get in the supermarket. I like helping her to bake. Cakes are more fun than tarts because she lets me lick the spoon. It tastes so sweet. Raw pastry does not taste very nice.

'Paul,' I yelled.

I stood there tied to the tree for what seemed like a whole day. The sun got higher and higher. I got hotter and hotter. I nearly fell asleep but I was too uncomfortable. The rope dug into my arms. I could not move at all without hurting my back even more. The tree dug into my shoulders. My shoulders are not like other children's shoulders. Mine stick out in tiny points.

Every so often I called, 'Paul, come back. Please.' But there was no sign of him.

I closed my eyes because the light from the sun was blinding me. I could feel my body being baked in the sun. Drips of water were running down my face and down my neck. I wanted to cry. I could feel tears burning under my eyelids.

I must have dozed off because after a while I heard a voice saying, 'Lucy, what are you doing?'

It was the girl next door peeping over the wall. Her name is Carol.

I tried to speak. But my mouth had dried out so I could not say a word. I opened and closed my mouth, begging her with my eyes to rescue me. Carol was my friend. She had to see that I was in trouble.

'Why are you tied up?' she asked.

I had no voice. Nothing would come out no matter how hard I tried to scream.

'Do you want me to untie you?' she asked.

I nodded hopefully.

'Is your mother inside?' she asked.

'No,' I tried to say. If my mother was inside, this would not have happened.

If my mother was inside, Paul would not have done this. Granny was inside.

Granny was supposed to be looking after us while Mum was at the shops. Granny could not look after herself. I don't know why Mum thought she would keep an eye on us.

Where had Paul gone? And why? Why had he left me to cook in the sun on the hottest day of summer?

'Wait a minute,' Carol said.

I could see her trying to pull herself up onto the wall. She seemed to be taking her time. She kept looking towards the kitchen window in my house. My mother did not like us using the wall to visit each other. So I suppose Carol was just being careful. But I wished she would hurry up.

She was on top of the wall now. I could see she was going to land on the sunflowers. I didn't care. Earlier I would have cared. I like flowers. Flowers remind me of music. Paul had planted the sunflowers and I really liked them. I liked the way their heads followed the sun as though they were drinking it in. Now I wished they would take all the heat from the sun so I could be cool again.

Carol walked carefully along the wall.

I knew she was pretending she was an acrobat in a circus. She wanted to be in a circus when she grew up, ever since my dad took us all to one. Carol had said that when she was sixteen, she was going to walk on a rope, high above the circus ring. She was going to run away from home and live with clowns and wild animals.

Paul said she would be the one to clean out the tigers' cage. They would never let her walk on a tightrope.

Carol said they would.

Paul said the tigers would eat her for dinner.

Now she was pretending she was carrying a pole to balance as she walked up and down the wall. She was wearing green shorts and a black T-shirt. On the T-shirt was a picture of a silver rabbit. Carol has a rabbit that lives in the house. Carol's mother would like the rabbit to live in the garden. But Carol says the rabbit likes to look at television. The rabbit's name is Bob.

'Hurry up,' I wanted to say. But still no words would come out of my mouth. The garden looked funny. It was all blurry, as though it was moving around. I closed my eyes.

'Don't fall asleep,' Carol said. 'Watch me. I'm fifty feet above the ground. Everyone is clapping and cheering.'

I wasn't clapping or cheering. A wave of sickness went over me. I felt my body beginning to sag. The ropes cut my arms. The bark of the tree was ripping my back. My head fell forward and the sun was even hotter on top of it. I could feel Carol beside me picking at the rope.

And then there was nothing.

Two

I heard a voice singing. It was like my voice only it was lighter and higher. And then I saw a face. It was like looking in a mirror. Almost like looking in a mirror. The face was mine but it was clearer. It had no scar on the chin. I have a scar on my chin where I fell when I was four. The eyes in the face looked into mine. I felt a wonderful wave of happiness.

The girl I was looking at smiled at me. Then she opened her mouth and she began to sing. High, high, high went her voice. They were the same sounds I had heard before I could see her. And then I opened my eyes.

I was lying on my face on the grass. Carol was screaming, 'Lucy, wake up! Lucy, Lucy!'

I wanted to go back to the face and the voice. I closed my eyes again.

'Oh God, you're bleeding,' Carol said. 'Oh no. Oh no. Oh no.'

The face that was like mine was in front of me again.

'Who are you?' I asked.

'I am your angel,' she said. 'Whatever happens, I will be with you. I will never leave.'

I could hear footsteps running but they sounded very far away. Carol was still screaming.

Then it was like a great black wave washing over me. I remember nothing more.

★

The next time I woke I was lying on my side in a bed. I did not recognise the room. There was a pink curtain around the bed. My dad was sitting on a chair facing me. He looked really sad.

'Dad,' I whispered.

He looked at me in surprise.

'You're awake,' he said. 'Oh, thank God, you're back with us.'

He held my hand and he called out, 'Nurse, nurse!'

For a moment I wondered where I was. My granny had been in a nursing home for six months. For a second I thought I must be there too. Granny went to a nursing home because she fell and broke her hip. She banged her head when she fell and she talked very strangely after that. One day she thought she was a goldfish. She opened and closed her mouth all the time.

Another day she thought she was the Pope. She blessed everyone who came to visit her. 'Bless you, my child,' she said to me. 'Bless you, my child,' she said to Paul. 'Bless you, bless you, bless you.'

Dad said, 'Oh, my God.'

Granny said, 'He is not here today. There is only me. I am here in his place. Bless you.'

Dad and Mum held hands and looked at each other. Paul giggled. I wanted to laugh too but Dad and Mum looked so sad.

Granny did not like the nursing home so she came to live with us.

★

I was not in Granny's nursing home. I was in hospital. That's what my dad now told me.

I wanted to ask him where Mum was. But my throat was too dry.

'Mum was here,' he said. Sometimes he just knows what I am going to say. 'Now she has gone home to get Paul to

15

bed. Then she is coming back. It's night now. Carol's mother is going to look after Paul so Mum can come back here to be with you. Carol found you in the garden,' he said.

Then I remembered the tree and the sun and the smell of the apples. I felt sick.

The nurse came running into the room.

'She's back with us then, is she?' she said. 'At last. Well, Miss Lucy Benedict, you gave us all a fright.'

'Is the doctor coming?' my dad asked.

The nurse nodded. She had a little silver watch pinned to her chest. She was holding my wrist and looking at her watch. That's what nurses do. I had been in hospital before when I was little. I did not really remember it. But I do remember a nurse holding my wrist.

'You gave your head quite a bang,'

the nurse said, touching my forehead. She shook her head. 'That is one big lump.'

'I feel sick,' I tried to whisper. My mouth was very dry.

'Thirsty,' I whispered.

'You may rinse your mouth with this,' the nurse said, giving me a cup of water. 'But don't swallow it.'

It tasted so cold and nice. Of course I drank it, even though she had told me not to.

'You have been in the sun too long. You have sunstroke,' she said.

I did not know what sunstroke was. I wanted to be sick. She gave me a little basin. My dad got a wet cloth and he wiped my face.

'Oh, Lucy, you must not drink,' the nurse said.

'Is she going to be all right?' I heard Dad ask.

I suppose he was afraid I would become like Granny. One day a goldfish. The next day the Pope.

'The doctor will be here in a minute,' the nurse said. 'This is normal. No need to worry.'

★

The doctor came in. My special doctor. His name is Dr Brown.

'Lucy, Lucy, Lucy,' he said as he came into the room. 'I'm glad you've decided to join us again. You had me very worried.'

I did not know what he meant. I had no choice. I did not mean to leave them by falling asleep in the sun and banging my head.

'Now, let's take a look,' he said. He sat down on the chair my dad had been sitting on. He used a little torch and he looked into my eyes. He shook his head.

'Can you tell me why you were tied to a tree?' he asked.

No, I couldn't. I was sick into the basin. This time the nurse wiped my face.

I never felt so sick in my whole life.

'My back hurts,' I tried to tell him.

'I know your back hurts,' Dr Brown said. 'I'm going to have to fix it all over again. But then you'll be as good as new.'

He looked at my dad.

'We'll have to wait a day or two before I can fix her back,' he said. 'That was quite a bang on her head. And she looks like she has sunstroke. We need to get her through this first.'

'What's sunstroke?' I asked.

'Too much sun,' the doctor said. 'From now on you are to play nice games with dolls or watch the television. There will be no more tree games for you, Lucy Benedict.'

He sounded cross but he was smiling at me.

I was his favourite patient. He told me that when I was little. He said I was the most important patient he had ever had.

I like playing with dolls, but Carol does not. She's my best friend. She likes climbing trees and walking on walls. She likes dancing. I like singing.

We both sing in school. Suddenly I remembered the angel.

'I saw an angel,' I said to Dr Brown.

'You are an angel,' he said to me.

'No.' I wanted him to listen. I wanted to tell him I had seen an angel and that she looked just like me. I wanted him to know. It was important.

'Now, stay on your side,' he said. 'I want to look at your back.'

Of course I would stay on my side. I could not lie on my back. I have never been able to lie on my back. My shoulders stand out in little points. When I try to lie on my back they dig into the bed. It hurts to lie on my back. Everyone has shoulder blades, but mine are special. That's what my dad and my mum say.

'You were nearly an angel,' my mum once said.

I think that maybe the points on my shoulders were meant to be wings.

When I go swimming I wear a T-shirt because I don't like people saying, 'What happened to your back?' There are some things you don't want to explain.

There are some things you don't know how to explain.

Three

Every year I go to see Dr Brown in the hospital. He is the one who fixed my back. After I was born, he tried to make my shoulders like everyone else's shoulders.

He says he did a good job of it. I don't know because I never saw what they looked like before he fixed them.

My dad said, 'Life is a gift. You are our gift, Lucy.'

'I'm a gift too,' Paul said.

'You're a monster,' I said to Paul.

'No, I'm not. You're the one with the monster back,' Paul said.

'She doesn't have a monster back,' my dad said.

'She has the back of an angel,' my mum said.

'She is an angel,' my dad said. 'Our angel.'

Paul stuck out his tongue at me when they weren't looking. He did lots of things when they were not looking. He stuck his finger in his nose and flicked it at me. I knew he wanted to be special. I knew he wanted Dad and Mum to tell him he was their angel too. But they were so busy telling me that they did not think of it.

I played his horrible games with him because I wanted him to be happy. I thought that the games would make him happy. I did not tell our parents when he held me on the ground so that my back was sticking into the hard earth. I did not tell on him when he farted in my face. I wanted him to be nice to me. But nothing I did made him nice to me. Instead it made him tie me up and leave me against the tree in the hot sun.

★

Now Dr Brown was looking at my back. I could feel him and the nurse taking the bandages off my shoulders.

I wished my mum would come back. I wanted her to be there. She always came with me when we went to see the doctor. She always held my hand and told me what was happening so that I would understand. Now I wanted her to be with me. I did not want her at home putting Paul to bed and kissing him goodnight. He had done this to me. He made my back sore. It was his fault. Everything was his fault. I started to cry.

'Lucy, it's all right,' Dad said, patting my hand.

I wanted my mum. She would hold my hand and make me feel safe. Sometimes only a mum can do that.

'It's going to be fine, Lucy,' Dr Brown said.

I could not see him because he was behind me. The nurse went, 'Tut tut.' I knew she did not like what she was seeing.

And then my mum arrived.

'Oh, Lucy,' she said as she came into the room. She kneeled down on the floor beside the bed. She kissed my face and my hands and then she held them.

'Don't cry,' she said. 'I know it is going to be all right. Isn't it, Doctor?'

'It is going to be all right,' Dr Brown said. 'We are going to give Lucy a day or two to get over the sunstroke and the bang on her head. Then we will whisk her to the operating theatre and make her back as good as new.'

'What's an operating theatre?' I asked.

'It's a special place where I make little girls better,' Dr Brown said.

'We will put on clean dressings,' the nurse said. I could see her lifting white things covered in blood. I hoped they had not come from my back. I hoped they were not the bandages.

'Look at me,' my mum said. 'Lucy, look at me.'

I did what she told me. I knew she did not want me to see what was happening. Sometimes when I look into her eyes I can see something else. She has lovely eyes. Big, dark brown eyes with long lashes. If I stare into them, I can feel all the bad things going away.

'That's better,' my mum said as I stopped crying. 'Everything is going to be fine again. Dr Brown will fix your back and you will be as good as new. Nearly as good as new.'

'Please don't leave me, Mum,' I said.

'I won't. Dad is going to go home. I will stay here for the night. Just like I did when you were little.' She smiled at me.

Parents can do two things at the same time. Just as she smiled at me, I could see her looking at Dr Brown as though she was asking him something.

'There, that's better,' said Dr Brown. 'Now, Nurse, I will leave you to put on a clean bandage while I talk to Mr and Mrs Benedict outside.'

I held Mum's hand tightly.

'I will be right back,' she said as she undid my fingers.

'Please don't leave me,' I begged.

'It's only for two minutes, Lucy,' she said. 'I need to know if you can swim this summer and if there are special things I have to give you to eat. I will be right back.'

She went outside with Dad and Dr Brown. I did not see why she could not be told those things while she was beside my bed holding my hand. If he had told her anything while I was there, I could remind her later if she forgot. But adults are like that. Sometimes they think there are things they have to talk about in private. Maybe they think that children will not understand.

'You are a very lucky little girl,' the nurse said to me. 'This could have been much worse. But Dr Brown will stitch you up and you will be fine again.'

'Aaaagh!' I let out a yell. I did not want to be stitched up. I wanted my back to get better without more stitches.

'Now, now,' she said. 'What are you crying about? He's going to make it just like it was.'

'I don't want stitches,' I said.

Paul had stitches in his knee once when he fell on the road. He screamed and screamed at the doctor's when he got two stitches. I was in the waiting room. I could hear him through the wall. When we got home and he finally fell asleep, Mum said to Dad, 'That was awful. I never want to go through that again.'

Dad shook his head. I was sitting on his knee. 'Think of poor little Lucy,' he said. 'She's so brave.'

I am not brave.

Sometimes we don't have any choice. Sometimes we just have to do what we're told because there is no other way out.

When I remembered that, I stopped yelling. It was not the nurse's fault that my back needed to be made better.

'Crying won't make anything better,' my mum once said.

She was right.

But sometimes you want to cry because things are just not fair.

I said that to my mum. She said, 'Lucy, life is not fair. You think it should be, but it isn't. Sometimes things happen that are so unfair that you don't know how you will recover. But then you say to yourself, it could be worse. It could always be worse. When you were a baby …'

'Yes, Mum?' I wanted her to tell me more.

She shook her head.

'It doesn't matter. All I want to say to you is this. When you feel so sad or so hurt that you cannot imagine feeling better again, you must remind yourself that you are lucky.'

I know that I am lucky. I have Mum and Dad and Paul and Granny, even if Granny is mad. And we live in a house with a little garden and an apple tree. I go to school down the road. And it is not far to the sea. And my friend Carol lives next door. And she has Bob her rabbit. Sometimes she lets me hold Bob. I like that. He is big and furry with long ears. I know that I am lucky. Not everyone has all of those things that I have.

At that moment I did not feel very lucky, lying on the hospital bed with the nurse at my back and my dad and mum outside the door with Dr Brown. But I suppose I *was* lucky because it was better than being tied to the tree in the sun. And if you look at life like that, things are always better than they might be.

Dad and Mum came back. Dad kissed me goodnight.

'Good night, Lucy,' he said. 'You lie there and rest and Dr Brown says he is going to make you much better. Better than you were before.'

He squeezed my hand.

Then he went home.

A nice camp bed was brought into my room. Mum helped the nurse to put on sheets.

'See?' Mum said. 'I'm going to be sleeping here right beside you. I'm not going to leave you. If you wake in the night, all you have to do is call me. I will be here.'

Her bed was beside mine. She held my hand while we went to sleep. I could see her face close to me. I closed my eyes.

Four

When I went to sleep I dreamed about the angel again.

She was in a place that was full of light. Her hair was fair like mine. Her eyes were brown like mine. My eyes are like my mum's. So were hers.

In my dream I walked with her in a place that was full of light.

She was dressed in white.

'Who are you?' I asked her.

She smiled.

She did not say anything.

'Will you sing for me?' I asked her.

She nodded. And then she began to sing.

I did not know the music that she was singing. It sounded like church music.

She sang and sang. Then I could hear another voice singing with her. At first I did not realise that it was my voice.

I suddenly woke up.

My mum was sitting beside me on the bed, stroking my face.

'Lucy,' she said gently.

I looked at her.

'You were singing in your sleep,' she said.

I smiled at her.

'Mum,' I said. 'There is this angel. I saw her earlier today when I fell from the tree onto the ground. She was dressed in white. She looks like me but has no scar on her chin.'

My mum touched the scar on my chin.

'You got that when you were three,' she said. 'You fell and bumped your chin on the toy box. Do you remember?'

'Yes. No.' I didn't want to talk about the scar on my chin. And anyway, I was four when I fell and got the scar. I wanted to tell her about the angel I heard singing. 'Mum. I dreamed about her again. She looks just like me.'

'It was just a dream, darling,' Mum said. 'Just a dream. Go back to sleep now.'

'But Mum, she sings just like me, only better. Her voice is …' I looked for a word. 'Sweeter,' I said.

'Just a dream,' my mum said.

Even though I knew it was a dream, it did not feel like one. It was very real. I wished my mum had not woken me up. I wanted to sing with this angel. I wanted my voice to be like hers.

I closed my eyes again. And then I slept a deep sleep. Until the morning.

★

When I woke in the morning I did not feel sick like I had the day before. My back still hurt. There was a lump on my forehead. But the sick feeling was gone. When I had a drink I was not sick.

Dad came in at ten o'clock.

'You look much better,' he said to me. 'Paul wanted to come in to see you too, but I said no. I said he had done enough damage and that you would not want to see him.'

I did want to see him though.

'I would like to see him,' I said.

'Well, we're not going to let him in here for a few days.'

'Maybe we should,' my mum said. 'It might do him some good to see what he did to Lucy.'

'He did not mean to,' I said. 'I mean, I know he tied me to the tree. But I know he did not mean to hurt me like this.'

'You're always so nice, Lucy,' my dad said.

No, I am not. Sometimes I am nice. But sometimes I am not. Some days I think everything is wonderful. And some days I do not. Some days I know Paul is nasty. But Paul is my brother. That makes him and me very close, even if he does do nasty things.

'Granny sends you her love,' Dad said.

I wondered if Granny really did send her love, or maybe it was a blessing from the Pope.

'It's funny,' Dad said. 'But Granny seems much clearer today. As if she is back to normal.'

'Really?' Mum asked. 'That's great.'

'Yes, really,' Dad said. 'She woke up

this morning and she knew where she was and why. She said we are very good to have her living with us and that she feels better.'

Mum smiled. 'I'm so glad,' she said.

'So am I,' my dad said. 'Let's cross our fingers that it lasts.'

I don't know why you cross your fingers when you hope something. Or sometimes Dad says, 'Touch wood.' That means that he hopes something is going to work out well.

'You know,' I said, 'it wasn't really Paul's fault. What happened, I mean. We were playing a game.'

'I know,' Mum said. 'It was really my fault. I was gone longer than I should have. I met someone at the shops and I had a coffee. I knew I should get back home. It was silly of me to leave Granny in charge. I wasn't thinking. I thought she would keep an eye on the two of you and that you would play.'

'It's all right,' Dad said. He was always saying that. 'You should be able to have coffee with a friend sometimes and not have to worry about what is happening at home.'

'It was Carol's mother,' my mum said. 'We could have coffee any day in our own houses and not stay down at the shops. I am really sorry.'

'It doesn't matter,' I said. This was not quite true. It did matter. I was in hospital. My back was hurting. I was going to have another operation.

'Sometimes things work out for the best,' my dad said. 'Don't forget that. It's not all doom and gloom.'

Five

Every year when I go to visit Dr Brown, he looks at my back, measures my height and sends me for an X-ray. Every year he nods slowly when he looks at the X-ray. He lays one from each year out on his desk. Then he lifts them one by one up to the light from the window. My mum and I look at them with him. My mum always tries not to look worried but I know she is. Every year he smiles at her and says, 'It's looking good.'

And then my mum smiles too.

He asks me about school and my
friends and what I am doing. I have to
swim twice a week and I love that. In
the summer we swim every day in the
sea. Dr Brown says the salt water and
the fresh air are good for children. I am
not allowed to play 'contact sports'.
Contact sports are games where you
can bump into other children. So I
swim and I sing.

Now I am in the hospital, lying in
bed. I don't know when I will swim
again. I feel very tired. I keep falling
asleep. When I do, the angel is there
and she sings for me.

Later in the day, Paul came to visit
me. He stood beside my bed and stared
at my face.

'Hi, Paul,' I said.

'Hi, sis,' he replied. That is what he
sometimes calls me when he is feeling
nice.

He handed me a bar of chocolate. 'I bought it with my own money,' he said.

'Thank you,' I said to him. He put it on the cupboard because I was lying on my side. It was too difficult to sit up because my back hurt. 'I will leave it here for you,' he said. 'It will melt if I put it on the bed.' He was sounding like a big brother. I liked that. I knew he cared for me.

He took a pack of cards out of his pocket. 'Want to play Snap?' he asked.

I said, 'Yes.' But I could not sit up, so we played on the bit of bed beside me. It is very difficult to play Snap lying down.

My mum left us to play while she went outside. I wondered if she was going for a cigarette or to talk to the nurses.

'Why did you not come back and untie me?' I asked Paul.

'I forgot,' he said. 'I am sorry. I found something. Then I forgot all about you and the tree and that I was to shoot you at dawn.'

'What did you find?' I asked as he said 'Snap' and took most of my cards.

'Remember I went inside to get my water pistol?' he asked.

'Yes,' I said. I only had about ten cards left. He was going to win.

'Well, when I got inside I remembered Dad had taken it from me last weekend because I shot Granny with it. Dad said that nice boys should not shoot their grandmothers. Remember?'

'Yes,' I said. Sometimes he was so slow in telling things. Of course I remembered. Granny had jumped back in her chair. There was water all over her very large chest. 'Is it blood?' she asked. 'He has shot me. My own grandson! And me the Pope! May God take me straight to heaven.'

Paul and I had both laughed. Then Dad said that it wasn't funny. He took the water pistol upstairs.

'Well, I went upstairs,' Paul continued.

'And I tried to think where Dad would hide the water pistol.'

'And did you find it?' I asked.

'I stopped looking,' Paul said.

'Why?'

'Because I found something else,' he replied.

'What did you find?' I asked.

'Have some more of my cards,' Paul said, giving me half the pack. It was nice of him to give me more cards. But I wanted him to tell me what he had found. He went and looked behind the curtains that were around my bed, to see if anyone was listening.

'Come back and tell me,' I said.

'Well,' he said, coming back and sitting close beside me on the bed. He sat so close that the sheet moved and all the cards fell on the floor.

'Oops,' he said, getting down off the bed and picking them up.

I wanted to scream. He can be so

annoying. First, he was the reason I was in hospital at all. Then he comes in to visit and starts to tell me something interesting. And then he gets distracted by anything at all.

'Well,' he said again. 'You know the tall cupboard in Mum and Dad's bedroom?'

'Yes,' I said. I was trying to be very patient and not tell him to jolly well hurry up. I was afraid that if I did hurry him, he would not tell me at all.

'You know the top shelf in it?'

I nodded. I did know the top shelf. I also knew there was a box up there. But it was too high up to reach. It was a shoe box. I often wondered what was in that box. It was a nice red box.

Once I asked Mum but she said, 'Oh, it's just old things,' and she changed the subject. She started talking about dinner and I knew she did not want me to ask about the box.

'Well,' said Paul. 'You know the box up there?'

'Yes,' I said.

'Well,' said Paul. 'I thought that maybe Dad put my pistol up there, so I got a chair and I climbed up.'

'And?' I asked. 'Was it there?'

'I don't know,' he said. 'Because I decided to look in the box instead …'

At that moment, Mum came around the curtain.

'Are you all right?' she asked me. 'You must not tire Lucy,' she said to Paul.

'I'm fine,' I said. I wanted to hear the rest of Paul's story. For the first time ever, I wanted my mum to go away and leave me with Paul.

'Your dad is downstairs,' Mum said to Paul. 'He's going to take you home now.'

'Dad's here?' I asked. 'Is he not going to come up and see me?'

'He will be back later,' Mum said. 'Now, Paul, put away the cards and say goodbye to Lucy.'

I really wanted to hear his story. But Paul looked at me and shrugged.

'I'll be back tomorrow,' he said.

'No,' Mum said. 'Lucy will be getting ready for her operation tomorrow. You can come back in a few days' time when Lucy is feeling better. Now, did you say sorry to her?'

'Yup,' Paul said. 'And I am sorry. I didn't mean to leave her there.'

'Tell her you will never tie her up again,' Mum said. 'Promise.'

'I promise,' Paul said with a sigh. But I knew he was imitating Mum's voice. 'I will never tie her up again.'

He looked at me with a grin. He bent close to my ear. 'I'll be back to tell you what I found. Now, do you want that bar of chocolate or can I have it?'

'You can have it,' I said. I knew he had bought it for himself because I only like dark chocolate, like my dad, and Paul knew that. He slipped the bar into his pocket, gave my hair a quick pull while Mum wasn't looking and then he was gone. I hoped he would remember what it was he had found in the box.

After a minute his head appeared between the curtains around my bed. He stuck his tongue out at me. And then he was gone again.

Six

I wasn't afraid of the operation. A bit of
me wanted everything to hurry up
because I wanted to go to sleep and
dream about my angel.

Dr Brown said, 'You will go to sleep,
Lucy. When you wake up, your back
will be a little sore for a few days. And
then you will feel like new.'

I didn't really want to feel like new. I
just wanted to feel like me again. I
know I don't feel like other people.
Other people don't have little wings on
their shoulders like I do. I see other

people's backs when they are swimming and their skin is smooth. My skin is bumpy and scarred on my back.

'You know, Lucy,' Dr Brown said, 'I was going to operate on you in the next year or so because I want to fix your spine. So instead of doing it when you are ten or eleven, I will do it now. This will be easier for you.'

Your spine is the long bone down the centre of your back. It is your backbone. It is made up of lots of little discs that move. Something happened to mine. That is why my back is a little different to everyone else's.

The sheets on my bed in the hospital are white. Mum brought me my yellow blanket so that the bed would look like the one at home. She said that she would be waiting by my bed when I came back from the operation.

'You'll be sleepy for a day,' she said. 'But I will sit here and be with you.'

She held my hand and gave me a kiss. 'I love you,' she said.

'Why is my back like this?' I asked her.

'I'll tell you when you're older,' she said. 'It's a long story.'

I like stories but I was too tired. I said goodbye to her and then I fell asleep.

At first the angel did not come but then I could hear her singing. I know it was a dream but it seemed so real. I was running through a field looking for her, following the sound of her voice. She sang such beautiful songs. She sang 'Ave Maria'. That is Latin. It is a church song. I love that song. Sometimes I sing it in church.

Her voice was high and pure. The notes she reached were higher than mine. Then I saw her. She was standing with her back to me in a field of flowers of every colour. She had little wings on her back, almost like mine but they were white. Her back had no scars. She was wearing a long white dress. The wings came out through it. She turned so that I could see her face.

It was my face.

Then suddenly I could hear Dr Brown's voice. He was calling my name.

'Lucy,' he said. 'You can wake up now. You are back in your bed. Your mother is here.'

Seven

Everyone was very happy with the operation. Dr Brown said, 'It went even better than I had hoped.'

My mum said, 'Lucy, I'm so proud of you. You are doing so well.'

My dad said, 'Lucy, you are so brave.'

The nurse said, 'Dr Brown is wonderful. I can't believe how good this looks.' She was looking at my back. I could hear the satisfaction in her voice. She was really pleased. 'It's a job well done,' she said.

Granny came in to see me.

'How is my little granddaughter?' she asked. That was nice because last month she had said I was a good priest and should be made a bishop.

'I'm fine, Granny,' I said. She looked nice. Her white hair was tied up with a clip. She was wearing a blue dress. She did not look mad at all. She was wearing pink lipstick.

'Granny,' I said. I thought I would tell her about the angel because she liked religion. After all, she had thought she was the Pope. 'I saw an angel,' I said to her.

'Oh, good,' said Granny. 'What was he like?'

This was great. She wanted to know about my angel. No one else did.

'She is a girl angel,' I said. 'She looks like me and she sings.'

'You sing beautifully,' Granny said.

'She sings better than me,' I told her.

Granny patted my hand. 'I'm not surprised,' she said with a smile. 'This must be your special angel.'

Granny said everyone has an angel but my angel is more special than anyone else's.

'Do you have an angel, Granny?' I asked.

'Yes, I do,' she said to me. 'Your granddad is my angel. He looks after me when I am sad or lonely.' Granddad died before I was born. I think it is nice that he looks after Granny.

Granny sat with me. She washed my face with warm water. Mum had gone home to have a bath and to change her clothes.

'I am not allowed to go swimming for a while,' I told Granny.

'You have to get strong again,' Granny said. 'Your back has to get better. Then you will be able to swim again. It won't be long until you can. Don't worry.'

Granny knows that I like to swim. She sits on the beach on a rug when I am in the sea. She wears sunglasses and she rubs cream into her skin. She says, 'Skin is a girl's best friend so you must look after it.' She wears a sun hat at the sea.

We used to live in another house in the country when I was little. I don't remember it very well. There was a field beside the house. In the mornings I could hear the birds singing in the trees. When I was little we moved to live near the sea. I like the sea.

'Granny,' I said, 'why did we move house when I was little?'

'You moved because your parents wanted to have a fresh start. When they saw the house you live in now, they knew it was the perfect place for you and Paul to be.'

'Why did they want a fresh start?' I asked. I did not really want to know the answer. I only asked because I wanted her to keep talking. When you are lying in bed and cannot do anything because you are sick, it is nice when people talk to you.

Before she could answer, Dr Brown came in with the nurse.

'Hello,' he said with a smile.

'I'm her grandmother,' Granny said, getting to her feet.

'Ah, yes, I remember,' Dr Brown said. 'I met you years ago when Lucy was little. It's nice to see you again. I'm just going to take a look at Lucy's back.'

Granny and Dr Brown shook hands.

'You are very good to my special little granddaughter,' Granny said.

Dr Brown said, 'It is my pleasure.'

Granny held my hand while the nurse removed the bandage from my back.

'This is looking very good,' Dr Brown said. 'We are going to get you up out of that bed today, Lucy Benedict. You can walk a little but you are not to get tired. This looks very good indeed.'

It hurt and my back felt funny. I did not like to move much because I was afraid of hurting it more. But after a while it was easier and I got used to it. I could walk to the window and look at the car park. I liked that because I could see the cars coming and going. Granny came with me. We watched for Mum coming back to the hospital.

Granny helped me back into bed. She fixed the pillows so I could sit up. When my lunch came on a tray, she cut my meat for me and told me to eat as much as I could.

'Do you want me to feed you?' she asked me. She put mashed potato onto the fork. I opened my mouth like a baby so that she could put it in.

'There,' she said. 'It's a long time since I've done that.'

'Did you feed me when I was a baby?' I asked her.

'Sometimes,' she said. 'Your mother needed a lot of help. It's difficult when you have babies. There is so much to do. It can be a very difficult time indeed.'

★

For the next few days I slept a lot. I walked to the window a lot. Mum and Dad and Granny took it in turns to stay with me. The most difficult thing was getting in and out of bed. They helped me. Mum slept with me every night. Some nights I dreamed about my angel. Some nights I did not dream at all.

Dr Brown came to see me every day. One day while the nurse was looking at my back, I heard Dr Brown say to my mum, 'She is eight years old. I think you should tell her.'

'You always said that we should tell her, right from the beginning,' my mum said.

They were outside the curtains. They moved away so that I could not hear any more.

'What did they mean?' I asked the nurse.

'I'm not sure,' she said. 'There now, we're finished. You know, your back is looking much better. You will be out of here in no time,' she added.

Paul came in that day. I was so pleased to see him. I missed him.

'It's very quiet at home without you,' he said.

'I'll be home soon,' I told him. 'The nurse says my back is nearly better. Mum, if you want to go and have some tea, Paul will stay with me and we can play cards,' I said to my mum.

'Thank you,' she said. 'I will go in a minute.'

I knew she wanted to be sure that Paul was going to be nice to me.

'Bob had babies,' Paul said.

'Bob?' I said. 'Bob? Carol's rabbit?'

'Yes. He's not a boy rabbit at all. He's a girl rabbit and he had ten babies.'

I thought about that. That was really exciting. I wondered if Carol's mother was excited too. I knew Carol would be.

'What did Carol's mother say?' I asked.

'I cannot repeat what Carol's mother said,' my mum said.

Paul looked at me and we both laughed. Then I said, 'Mum, do you think I could have one of Bob's rabbits?'

I would love a rabbit. Bob is so nice to hold. He just sits in my arms and I can kiss his head.

'We will see,' Mum said. 'I think I will leave you two for a little bit. But you are to be nice to Lucy,' my mum said to Paul. 'You are to be gentle and kind.'

'I'm always gentle and kind,' Paul said. He winked at me. We all knew he was not always gentle and kind.

Mum said, 'I will go downstairs and get coffee. I won't be long. Now play nicely.' She looked at us both. I know she did not trust Paul.

Paul got out the cards. I did not want to play Snap. I wanted him to tell me what he had found in the cupboard.

'Are you sure you will be all right?' Mum said to me.

'We will be fine,' Paul said as he dealt the cards.

Mum went outside. I could hear her footsteps on the floor as she walked away.

'Well, Paul,' I said. 'Tell me.'

'Carol said we can each have a rabbit,' Paul said. 'But you are not to tell Mum. We will wait until they are a little bigger. I'm going to make them a little house in the garden because Mum won't let them in the house.'

'Oh, that's great,' I said. I was really pleased. I would love to have a rabbit and now I was going to be given one of Bob's babies.

I was so busy thinking about the rabbit and what name I would give it that I nearly forgot what I really wanted to know.

'Paul, tell me, please.'

'Tell you what?' he asked.

'What you found in the box.'

'What box?' He looked puzzled.

'You know. You told me you climbed up in Mum and Dad's cupboard and you found something in the box. The shoe box. The red box. Remember? You were looking for your water pistol and you looked in the box instead.'

'Oh, yes. I forgot.' He laughed. 'Look. I brought this to show you.' He stood up and started digging in his pockets. 'Don't tell Mum I showed you this or she will know I was looking in the box.' He took something out of one of his pockets. 'Look.' He passed it to me. It was a photograph.

I took it from him and I looked at it. It was a picture of two babies. They were lying back to back, dressed in white.

'There are lots of pictures like these,' Paul said.

I looked at it again. 'So?' I said. I couldn't understand what he thought was so interesting about it.

'In all the pictures the babies are lying like that,' he said. 'Back to back. Look, their dress is just one dress …'

'What is that?' It was Mum. She had come back into the room. We had not heard her.

Paul tried to take the photo from me and slip it under the bedclothes.

'Show me that,' Mum said.

I passed it to her. Paul was looking worried.

Mum held the photo and she looked at it. Then she looked at Paul.

'Please don't be angry,' I said to her. 'I asked him to show it to me.'

'I am not angry,' she said. 'You should not have gone looking in that box,' she said to Paul. 'But I am not angry. I should have told you about this a long time ago. But I was so sad that I did not want to talk about it.'

Paul and I looked at each other. I think we both knew that she wanted to tell us something important.

'What is it, Mum?' I said. 'Please tell us.'

Eight

This is the story my mum told Paul and me.

'Your Dad and I always thought we were very lucky. We had Paul soon after we were married. He was a wonderful, healthy baby. Then two years later we had twins. Twin girls. They were healthy too but they were different. Something had happened while they were inside me. They did not separate the way twins usually separate. They stayed joined together at the shoulders. When they were born we were very surprised. We did not know such a thing could happen. They were so beautiful. Two beautiful little girls. But we knew that they could not live like that. Their shoulders were joined together. We knew that some time they would have to be separated. We wanted them to have a full and happy life. We wanted them to live properly. Dr Brown looked after them. Dr Brown said that he would separate them.'

At that moment, Dr Brown came into the room.

He sat on the bed beside me. He took the photograph from my mum and looked at it.

'I remember this well,' he said. 'This was how I first saw you, Lucy.'

He handed the photograph back to my mother. I took it from her and looked at it again. One of those babies was me. I wondered which one. They were so little and so sweet. And one of them was me.

This was a surprising thought.

'I decided to operate when you were just over a year old,' he said. 'It seemed a good time to do it, while you were still very young. Everything went to plan. We were all very happy. We separated you and your twin sister. But two days later she became very ill. And then she died.'

'Why did you never tell me?' I asked.

'We wanted you to think that you were special just because you are you,' my mum said. 'And you *are* special just because you are you. We did not want you to grow up sad, knowing that your twin had died. Maybe we should have told you. Dr Brown always said we should tell you. But I could not bring myself to do it.'

'It's all right, Mum,' I said. 'Please don't be unhappy.' She looked really sad.

'I wanted to do what was right for you,' she said to me. 'It's very difficult sometimes to know what is the right thing to do.'

I lay on my bed in the hospital. Now I had answers to lots of questions. I knew why my back was different to everyone else's back. I knew that once I had a twin sister who had been joined to my back. But I did not feel sad at all. It was good to have answers. It was good to know who the angel was and that she would always be with me.

'What was her name?' I asked.

'Her name was Lily,' my mum said.

I closed my eyes. Lily. I tried the word inside my head. Then I said it aloud. 'Lily.'

Lily is a lovely name. I loved knowing her name. I loved knowing that I was special and that so was she. My mind was full of knowing that I knew Lily and that Lily knew me. I loved knowing that once we were joined together, that we would always be special to each other even though she had died.

Paul took my hand. I think he thought I was sad.

'You have me,' he said. 'I'm your brother. I will look after you.'

We smiled at each other. Now we both knew the truth. Truth is good. It explains things. I was glad they had told us. Later I would tell him about the angel. And he would know that Lily would always be with us, singing and dancing in my dreams.

And I would grow up and I would sing, not just for me but also for Lily. My special angel would always be there at my back.

OPEN DOOR SERIES

SERIES ONE

Sad Song by Vincent Banville

In High Germany by Dermot Bolger

Not Just for Christmas by Roddy Doyle

Maggie's Story by Sheila O'Flanagan

Jesus and Billy Are Off to Barcelona
by Deirdre Purcell

Ripples by Patricia Scanlan

SERIES TWO

No Dress Rehearsal by Marian Keyes

Joe's Wedding by Gareth O'Callaghan

The Comedian by Joseph O'Connor

Second Chance by Patricia Scanlan

Pipe Dreams by Anne Schulman

Old Money, New Money by Peter Sheridan

SERIES THREE

An Accident Waiting to Happen
by Vincent Banville
The Builders by Maeve Binchy
Letter from Chicago by Cathy Kelly
Driving with Daisy by Tom Nestor
It All Adds Up by Margaret Neylon
Has Anyone Here Seen Larry?
by Deirdre Purcell

SERIES FOUR

The Story of Joe Brown by Rose Doyle
Stray Dog by Gareth O'Callaghan
The Smoking Room by Julie Parsons
World Cup Diary by Niall Quinn
Fair-Weather Friend by Patricia Scanlan
The Quiz Master by Michael Scott

SERIES FIVE

Mrs Whippy by Cecelia Ahern
The Underbury Witches by John Connolly
Mad Weekend by Roddy Doyle
Not a Star by Nick Hornby
Secrets by Patricia Scanlan
Behind Closed Doors by Sarah Webb

SERIES SIX

Lighthouse by Chris Binchy
The Second Child by John Boyne
Three's a Crowd by Sheila O'Flanagan
Bullet and the Ark by Peter Sheridan
An Angel at My Back by Mary Stanley
Star Gazing by Kate Thompson